MEET THE MEMBERS OF THE
SPY Society

MOLLIE KILBURN
Brainy Mollie uses her smarts to find the perfect solutions to tricky problems.

CAMILLE WU
Actress extraordinaire Camille is ready at a moment's notice to take on a dramatic new persona.

NINA CRANDALL
Fashionable Nina knows how to dress the part of fabulous spy.

TATUM SCOTT
Gadget girl Tatum can figure out how absolutely anything works.

SPY Society

Disguised & Dangerous

by Jane B. Mason and Sarah Hines Stephens

Illustrated by Craig Phillips

SCHOLASTIC INC.

New York Toronto London Auckland
Sydney Mexico City New Delhi Hong Kong

ISBN 978-0-545-37469-9

12 11 10 9 8 7 6 5 4 3 2   11 12 13 14 15/0

Printed in the U.S.A.   40
First printing, October 2011

Designed by Jennifer Rinaldi

her dog's leash and launched into a throat-clenching, staggering death scene. Several seconds later she flopped on a patch of grass next to their favorite bench and pretended to be dead.

Camille's friends burst into a fit of giggles. "Bravo," Nina cheered. She reached out a hand to help the actress back up. "But this is hardly your bitter end. You never get anything lower than a B plus. None of us do," she pointed out. "So you'll keep your drama. I'll keep doing costumes for the drama department. Tatum and I will keep playing volleyball. And Mollie will keep plowing her way through every book that's ever been written."

Camille brushed herself off and picked up the end of Tallulah's leash. "You really think so?"

"I know so," Tatum answered. "We're fine." She watched a couple of kids play on the jungle gym. "What I don't know is why the Sports Packers don't seem worried at all."

"I know!" Nina agreed. "It seems like the jocks are always goofing off in study hall."

Mollie nodded. "I never see them in the library, either."

"Right. They never work, unless you count working out," Nina said. "So how are they going to stay on their teams?"

"No idea," Camille said with a shrug. She was about to suggest they keep walking when she noticed a stylish handbag sitting all alone on a nearby bench.

"Hey, what's that?" She pointed to the large leather handbag. The bag was beautiful and had a fancy-looking logo stitched into the side.

"Wow," Nina cooed. "That is some buttery-looking leather." She reached to pick the bag up.

"Don't touch it!" Tatum warned, her dark eyes flashing. "We have no idea what's inside that thing."

"Now who's being dramatic?" Camille raised an eyebrow and looked around to see if anyone was nearby. Maybe someone left the bag by accident. She saw kids on the jungle gym and a few assorted parents. Nobody else.

"How do you think it got here?" Mollie asked.

"No idea," Tatum replied. "Which is exactly the point."

"Don't be such a worrywart," Nina said. "Besides, we can't just leave it here. Someone must want it back." She picked it up. "Oh my gosh. Feel this." She caressed the leather.

Nina slipped the bag's strap onto her shoulder and Camille could see that her fashionable friend was instantly in love. The leather was a beautiful shade of purply brown, like something that would be called "mushroom" or "sandstorm" in a magazine. And despite the bag's large size, Camille noticed it rested perfectly against Nina's side. Whoever designed it definitely knew what he or she was doing!

Camille smiled at her friend. Nina was super into fashion and knew her accessories. But the bag was still a mystery. Camille was certain it hadn't been there when she'd pretended to die just a few minutes ago. And she hadn't seen anyone walk by them on the trail, either. She looked around again. Nobody. Just a silver sports car idling at the curb.

"Maybe we should just leave the bag where we found it," Camille suggested.

"Somebody might take it," Nina responded, flipping her long hair over her shoulder. "We need to rescue it so we can return it."

Nina unzipped the bag and peeked inside. Camille expected her to pull out a wallet or a phone . . . regular handbag stuff. Stuff that would help them return the bag. Instead, she pulled out a makeup bag.

"Definitely belongs to a woman," Nina confirmed. She handed the small fabric pouch to Tatum, then reached in again and pulled out a pair of oversized sunglasses.

"Oooh, those are fabulous," Camille said, snatching them and slipping them on. She raised her chin, striking a pose. "How do I look?"

"Maahhhvelous," Nina replied before diving back in. It was so big her whole head practically disappeared inside.

Tatum reached over and pulled the bag off Nina's shoulder. "Let's not unpack here." She dropped the makeup case back in, zipped the bag shut, and set the whole thing back on Nina's shoulder.

"Let's take it back to Camille's house," Tatum said. "Maybe we can find some sort of ID inside and return it." She started down the path. Nina followed, cradling the leather bag like a baby. Mollie wasn't far behind.

Glancing back, Camille saw the tinted window of the sports car roll up.

"Come on, Camille!" Tatum shouted from up ahead.

Camille shivered. She had the feeling that she and her friends were being watched. *Cut the drama!* she told herself. *You're being ridiculous*. But as the silver car pulled into traffic, Camille found herself walking faster than Tallulah to catch up with her friends.

Chapter 2

FIFTEEN MINUTES later the girls were crowded into Camille's room.

"What do you think the *S*s stand for?" Tatum asked.

Nina wrinkled her eyebrows. "What *S*s?"

"The logo," Tatum said, turning the bag around. Sure enough, two *S*s were stitched into the side.

Nina peered at the letters. Were they the designer's initials? It didn't look familiar, and she knew practically every designer. She pulled items out of the mystery bag and set them on the bed one by one. First came the makeup pouch. Then a fancy journal with a matching pen.

"It has the same logo!" Mollie pointed out. She ran a finger over the swirling *S* design.

"They probably came with the bag," Nina reasoned as she reached in to grab the next item. Her hand slipped into a small side pocket and she pulled out a silver MP3 player.

"Excellent," Camille cried, reaching for the player. She shoved the earbuds in and switched it on. "Let's see what kind of music this lady likes!" she said loudly. She bopped around the room like a crazy robot.

The other three girls giggled at their friend's antics. "So what is it?" Mollie finally asked, her green eyes sparkling with laughter. "What are you listening to?"

"Nothing," Camille replied, waving her arms and stopping short. "I think it's broken. Or maybe it needs charging."

Nina continued to rummage through the bag. There was something folded up at the bottom . . . something big. Her fingers closed around it and she pulled it out, gasping. It was a long oatmeal-colored trench coat with silver stitching.

"Oh my gosh!" Nina squealed. She stood up and slipped her arms through the sleeves.

Mollie looked up. "That's gorgeous."

Nina buttoned the coat and went to check herself out in the full-length mirror. It fit her perfectly and felt like a million dollars.

Tatum dumped the bag over, still searching for some sort of ID. "Girls, we got nothing," she announced. "No wallet, no cell phone, no ID. There's no contact information here at all." She rubbed her mocha brown chin thoughtfully.

"I wonder if the Ss are initials," Camille offered.

Tatum picked up the notebook and looked through it. The pages were all blank. Everything looked brand-new.

"How are we going to return this stuff to the owner if we don't know anything about her?" Mollie wondered.

"We can be sure she has great taste—and is exactly my size," Nina said as she pulled up the collar on the coat. "What else is there to know?"

"Who the stuff actually belongs to?" Mollie suggested.

She sifted through the makeup and picked up a lip gloss.

Tatum pulled the lid off the pen and scribbled in the book. Nothing appeared. "Maybe she was throwing all of it away. This pen isn't working, either, which is weird. I mean, it looks like it's never been used."

Nina and Camille were posing by the mirror, admiring their reflections. "No way was somebody tossing this coat, or the glasses," Nina protested.

"Check it out! We look like spies!" Camille cried, slinking around the room like she was undercover.

Tatum squinted at her. "Let me see those." She pulled the sunglasses off her friend's face and slipped them onto her own.

"I hope she was getting rid of all this. I don't want to give it back," Nina confessed. She had never seen such a cool trench, much less worn one. "It feels like this coat was made for me."

Behind her, Tatum was hunched over the notebook. "Maybe it was," she said mysteriously.

Something in Tatum's voice made Nina stop and turn. "What did you say?" she asked.

"I said maybe it was made for you," Tatum repeated. "I think I just discovered something!" She pulled off the sunglasses and handed them to Nina, who sat down on the edge of the bed.

Nina looked at the notebook through the lenses and was shocked to see a message there:

use what you find. Employ your powers for good causes, not evil deeds. Together you will solve many mysteries.
Good Luck!

"I think we were supposed to find this bag," Tatum pronounced.

Nina passed the glasses to Mollie and Camille so they could see the message, too.

"See the bold letters?" Tatum asked. "S-P-Y S-O-C-I-E-T-Y. That must be what the *S*s stand for."

"Spy Society?" Nina echoed. "What's that supposed to mean?"

Camille tapped her foot on the carpet. "Um, a society of spies?"

"Right, but—"

"Listen," Tatum said, interrupting. "I think we were supposed to find this bag, and I think we're supposed to use it. *We're* the Spy Society."

Mollie laughed her raspy laugh. "I'm loving this crazy spy thing, but let's face it: Ridgewood is not exactly a hot spot for intrigue and espionage!"

"She's right," Camille groaned. "We've got nobody to spy on. The real mystery is why anyone would give this stuff to us!"

Chapter 3

TATUM PULLED her phone out of her pocket for the tenth time. Eight eighteen, one minute later than the last time she checked. She shifted her weight from one foot to the other and leaned against the auditorium door. Where was everybody?

When they left Camille's last night, Nina had put everything back into the giant leather bag—including the trench—and handed it to Tatum.

"You should take it," Nina had said. "If the pen and glasses are good for sending secret messages, who *knows* what the rest of the things do. You're our gadget girl. I think you should take a closer look."

The other girls had nodded their agreement, and Camille had even relinquished the sunglasses.

"I'll take good care of it," Tatum had promised. She'd stayed up past midnight fiddling with the stuff, and had made some impressive discoveries. The silver stitching in the trench coat was for more than just looks—it was actually wire! The makeup bag had contained two "devices"—a powder compact and a fancy lip gloss. Tatum already knew that the sunglasses helped them read whatever was written in the book with the pen that "didn't work." It was possible that the dark lenses were useful for other things, too.

It had been tempting to take everything apart. Part of her was dying to get out her tiny ratchet set and start removing miniature screws. But she wasn't 100 percent sure that she'd be able to put everything back together in exactly the right way. And then they would *never* know how the stuff worked.

Tatum stomped her sneakered feet impatiently. She checked her phone: eight twenty-one. School would start in nine minutes. Looking around, she spotted

Mollie and heaved a sigh of relief.

"Finally!" Tatum cried as her friend hurried over.

"Sorry," Mollie said. "Alarm fail. Where's everyone else?"

"Late!" Tatum complained. "I'm not going to have time to debrief everyone on our spy goods before first period. But I'm glad you're here, at least." She reached into her bag and pulled out the MP3 player. "I spent a long time checking out the trench coat and compact, so I barely got to this," she explained. "But I'm pretty certain there's more to this music player than meets the eye."

Mollie took the player, clearly intrigued.

"Morning," Nina panted as she and Camille hurried over. "Sorry we're late. I was trying to finish my homework. Brrrr. It's cold today!"

"Maybe this will help," Tatum said, holding up the trench for her to put on.

"Ooooh, really?" Nina asked, her blue eyes shining.

Tatum nodded. "Of course. It was made for you, remember? And believe me, it goes beyond fashion. The silver thread is wire. I'm pretty sure it's for recording but I don't know exactly how it works. Your mission is to figure it out."

Nina nodded while Tatum handed the sunglasses to Camille. She pointed out a tiny screw in the sunglass hinge. "This is some kind of dial," Tatum said. "I think the glasses can be set to different modes; we just have to figure out what the modes do."

Camille fiddled with the dial for a moment, then frowned. "Even if we figure out how this stuff works, how are we supposed to know what to use it for?" She heaved an exasperated sigh.

Suddenly Mollie's eyes widened. She had the earbuds in and was looking past her friends at something down by the double doors. She put a finger to her lips and pointed with her other hand. "What the . . ."

Travis Brandt, Lincoln's hulking football star, was talking to Mabel Brodie. Mabel was a seventh-grade Nerd Herd girl. Travis was a major figure in the Sports Pack. Definitely not a pair that usually hung out . . . and Travis looked mad.

Tatum strained to hear what they were saying but they were just out of earshot . . . until Mollie shoved one of the earbuds into her ear. All of a sudden Tatum could hear the conversation, clear as day. The MP3 was a listening device!

Unfortunately, Travis and Mabel's conversation was pretty much over. "You'll regret it if you don't" was all Tatum heard before Travis stalked into the building.

Mabel stared after Travis, silent but obviously shaken. Nina hurried over to the frightened-looking geek, the other girls not far behind. When they got closer Tatum could see that even Mabel's freckles had gone pale. She was seriously freaked.

"Are you okay, Mabel?" Nina asked.

Mabel's head jolted up in surprise. She stared mutely at the four girls for several seconds. "I'm fine," she finally blurted. "I'm . . . fine." She hoisted her heavy backpack onto her shoulder and scurried away.

"That was weird," Mollie announced.

"Totally weird," Nina agreed.

The bell rang, and Camille groaned. "First period

math," she said. "My least favorite class of the day." Camille disliked math as much as she loved drama.

As the girls headed into the building, Tatum discreetly handed the makeup bag to Mollie. "Nice work with the MP3," she said. "Now see what you can make of this."

Chapter 4

"SEE YOU at lunch," Mollie called as she headed toward her own math class—seventh-grade geometry. Mollie loved being known as a math whiz, but she didn't like not being able to take sixth-grade math with her friends.

Making her way down the hall, she pondered the scene she'd just witnessed. Travis and Mabel were definitely not friends, and they were definitely not having a casual conversation. So what were they talking about . . . and why?

Mollie stepped into her classroom and found her seat in the back. Trying to look low-key, she opened the cosmetic bag. She'd checked out the lip gloss the day before at Camille's house, but hadn't really had a chance to figure out what its ordinary appearance might be hiding. Holding it in her hand, she turned it over. She was hardly a makeup expert—she never wore the stuff—but it felt extra . . . heavy. She examined the top of the lid, then unscrewed the wand and grinned. The wand was fatter than usual, and Mollie was pretty sure the sparkle she saw was not for preventing chapped lips. It looked like a lens. If her guess was right, this tube of gloss had photographic capabilities!

Glancing up, Mollie watched Mabel come in with her best friend and fellow Nerd Herder, Erika Roderick. Looking anxious, the twosome whispered together over a desk two rows ahead.

Mollie didn't have time to listen in on what they were saying before Ms. Hawthorn called the class to order. "Take your seats, please," she announced. "We have a lot to cover after our quiz."

A chorus of groans went up at the mention of a quiz. Ms. Hawthorn clucked the class to silence, stood, and handed a small pile of quiz sheets to the first person in each row. "The sooner you start, the sooner you'll be finished," she said logically. Ms. Hawthorn was always logical.

Mollie was fourth in her row to get a copy of the quiz, and she immediately scanned the questions. There were twenty, all about angles. It didn't look hard.

The rest of the class settled down and waited for the word to get started—all except the Bubble Gums in the back row.

The Bubble Gums were the popular girls at Lincoln. They got their name from the fruity wads of gum they were always chomping. Hilary Black and Kayla Huff were the Bubble Gum queens. And right now they were whispering and giggling two seats behind Mollie.

"Jenna gave me the name of this amazing DJ," Kayla said. "I'm going to call him right after school."

Mollie ignored her quiz for a second and listened. The girls were talking about Kayla's birthday party loudly enough for Mollie to hear without the MP3. Rumor had it that the entire seventh grade was going to be invited to the party, but Mollie didn't believe it. Only the popular kids—the Bubble Gums and the Sports Packers—would probably end up on the guest list.

"Awesome," Hilary replied, flipping her blonde hair over her shoulder.

"It is going to be—"

"You may begin," Ms. Hawthorn instructed, giving the girls a sharp look. "You have fifteen minutes to complete the problems."

Mollie tuned out the Bubble Gums and got started. She moved easily through the first few problems and was just getting started on the fourth when her pencil lead broke. She headed to the front of the room to resharpen.

That's weird, Mollie thought as she passed Mabel's desk. Mabel was using scratch paper for her quiz. That would have been normal during a hard test. Sometimes it was helpful to have extra space to make notes and work out problems. But this wasn't a hard test. What was she scribbling? Mollie squinted to get a better look. At the same moment, Mabel looked up. Instead of smiling shyly, like she usually did, Mabel hunched down awkwardly, blocking the paper from Mollie's view.

Mollie wasn't sure what was going on, but she had a feeling it was something a member of the Spy Society should be paying attention to. She sharpened her pencil, walked back to her desk, and finished her quiz as quickly as she could. When she got to the last problem, she pressed extra hard on her pencil. *Snap!* The lead broke for a second time.

"Not again!" she exclaimed quietly, hoping the kids around her could hear. She feigned a sigh and silently thanked Camille for teaching her a few dramatic skills. Then she pulled the lip gloss out of the makeup bag.

At the front of the room, Mollie sharpened her pencil again. On the way back, she unscrewed the gloss and pulled out the wand. She held it up to her lips as she passed Mabel's desk. Aiming the teeny sparkling lens she hoped was hidden in the tip of the gloss in the Mabel's direction, Mollie casually pressed the button on the lid. *Click!*

I hope this is how I'm supposed to work this thing, she thought, grimacing and hurrying back to her desk. She didn't really know how to use actual lip gloss, much less a high-tech spy gadget that looked like it!

"Time's up, class." Ms. Hawthorn's voice seemed extra loud as Mollie slid into her seat. Her palms were sweaty, and she could feel her heart thudding in her chest. Taking a deep breath, she screwed the lip gloss shut and slipped it into her pocket. Geometry had never been so exciting.

Chapter 5

CAMILLE SET her tray on the lunchroom table and took a seat. "It just doesn't make sense," she declared. "Why would Erika Roderick be invited to Kayla's birthday party?"

Tatum looked up from her sandwich, her dark eyebrows knit together. "What are you talking about?"

Camille tilted her head toward the lunch line, where a throng of students waited to get food. "I just overheard Hilary asking Erika if she got her invitation."

Tatum chewed thoughtfully. "She was probably teasing her. That Bubble Gum queen loves to make sure everyone knows how popular she is."

Camille spooned up a bite of soup. Hilary and Kayla

were the most popular girls in seventh grade and made sure that nobody forgot it. But Camille wasn't convinced that Hilary was teasing. "I don't think so," she insisted. "Hilary was going on about how it was going to be as much fun as Jeremy's pool party. She was like, 'Erika, you know you had a great time at Jeremy's!' Except that doesn't make any sense, either. What would Erika be doing at Jeremy's?"

"A Nerd Herder at a Bubble Gum party," Tatum said, squinting at the popular kids. The Bubble Gums were laughing, talking, and eating at the big table in the middle of the room, like they always did.

Then, out of the blue, Kayla got up and walked over to the Nerd Herders. She smiled at Mabel and Erika and started passing out envelopes. "Look," Tatum whispered, aghast. "Kayla is handing out invites to the entire Herd!"

Camille stared in amazement. "Maybe her mom made her invite the whole class?" she suggested.

"Highly unlikely," Tatum replied. "Why would any mom want eighty-five kids at her house?"

"This is definitely bizarre," Tatum said. "But we can't waste time trying to understand seventh-grade politics. We've got more important stuff to figure out—like how our spy gear works! Did you discover anything new about the glasses?"

Camille shook her head. "Not yet. We were rounding fractions in math, and I had to pay attention—it's totally confusing!" She made a face just as Mollie showed up with a slice of pizza and a salad.

Mollie squeezed behind Tatum's chair and sat down in the corner. Taking a quick bite of pepperoni, she shoved her tray aside and opened her laptop. "Just keep doing what you're doing," she whispered mysteriously.

Tatum raised an eyebrow but didn't comment.

"The plot thickens," Camille said, stifling a giggle.

Keeping her hands under the table, Mollie pulled out the lip gloss and removed a piece to reveal a memory stick. She plugged the stick into a slot on the side of her laptop. She tapped a few keys. Moments later, the picture of Mabel's desk that Mollie had taken during the quiz popped up.

"I have a feeling I'm looking at our first clue," Tatum said, leaning in.

"Take a look, but act casual," Mollie cautioned. She zoomed in while her friends squeezed around her.

"That's a clue?" Camille whispered. "It looks like a math quiz."

"It's two math quizzes," Mollie corrected. "Two *identical* math quizzes. I'm pretty sure Mabel is cheating."

The three girls fell silent, their gazes inconspicuously moving toward the Nerd Herd table. Despite the fact that she'd just been invited to one of the biggest parties of the year, Mabel looked miserable.

"Don't stare!" Mollie whispered. The girls pulled their eyes back to the computer screen.

"But why?" Camille asked the obvious question. "Mabel is practically the smartest kid in the whole school. She doesn't need to cheat."

Several tables away, rowdy Sports Packers perched on their chairs. Travis tossed a handful of popcorn across the table at Frank. A moment later Frank was on his feet, returning fire.

A huge laugh erupted from the Pack and more popcorn went flying. Then Mabel leaped to her feet and bolted out of the cafeteria, holding her stomach. Her friend Erika was right behind her.

Chapter 6

NINA TIGHTENED the belt on her new favorite coat and reached for the door handle. Her stomach was growling, and she was late for lunch! But before she could exit the bathroom stall, the outside door opened and the sounds of worried voices filled the room.

"We can't let anyone find out!" someone was saying.

Nina froze, trying to place the voice.

"That's why we have to go," said a second girl.

Mabel Brodie, Nina thought. *The first voice was Mabel Brodie's.* No sooner did she figure that out than Mabel started to cry. Nina felt a wave of sympathy, followed by a wave of guilt for eavesdropping on such a private conversation. But it wasn't her fault she happened to be in the bathroom stall!

"It's going to be okay," the second voice said. Nina was pretty sure it was Mabel's friend Erika.

Mabel sniffled and Erika stepped into a stall to get her some toilet paper. Mabel blew her nose like a trumpet.

"I'm scared," she said when she was finished blowing. "But I don't know what else to do. Travis said this is the only way. I . . . I just can't do it anymore."

Nina peered through the crack in the door. She couldn't see the girls—they were too far over—and she had no idea what they were talking about. But whatever it was sounded intriguing! She inhaled silently and waited for more.

The door opened again, and Nina heard the distinct sound of snapping gum. Even this far down the row she could smell the grape double bubble.

"Oh, hiii," Hilary said. Her sugary voice dripped with mock sincerity. Nina felt a flash of anger. Why did the popular girls have to be so cruel?

"You don't look so good, Mavis," Kayla added, getting

her name wrong. "I hope you're not sick. I'd hate for you to miss my party."

"I'll be fi-fine," Mabel stammered before clearing her throat. "See you there," she added more clearly.

"Yeah, see you," Erika said, sounding a little annoyed.

The Nerd Herders left, and Nina was about to make her own exit when she reconsidered. Who knew what she might hear if she stayed put . . . and invisible . . . behind the stall door?

Nina dropped her hand to her side, slipping it into her trench coat pocket. Her fingertips brushed against something she hadn't felt before—something round and smooth. An extra button, maybe? It was hard to tell without taking the coat off and turning the pocket inside out. She certainly wasn't going to do *that* right now.

Whatever it was, it was sewn securely into the lining. Nina pushed on it while Hilary and Kayla preened in front of the mirror.

"I'm doing the whole house up in black and white," Kayla said excitedly. "My mom said she doesn't care as long as I pay for it. I'm so glad we're getting that extra cash!"

"I know," Hilary agreed. Nina could picture her flipping her perfectly highlighted hair like she did every chance she got. "Our good grades are paying off in more ways than one!" The girls erupted into a fit of giggles.

In the stall Nina wrinkled up her nose and stuck out her tongue. It just figured that the snotty, spoiled, gum chewers were getting cash from their parents for making good grades. Nina's mom insisted that doing well in school was its own reward—and it was. But a little money would be nice, too.

Suddenly Nina felt tired of listening to the two girls gloat, and opened the door. The minute she stepped out, the Bubble Gums got quiet.

"Oh, hi. It's Nina, right?" Hilary finally said. She was acting like she didn't really know Nina, even though they'd gone to the same elementary school for years.

"Yeah," Nina said, enjoying the worried expressions on the girls' faces. "Hi, Hilary. Hi, Kayla."

The Bubble Gums exchanged looks in the mirror

while Nina washed her hands.

"Cool coat, Neen," Hilary said, reaching out to touch the smooth fabric.

"Is it designer?" Kayla asked.

"Something like that," Nina replied as she shut off the faucet. Tossing the damp paper towel into the trash, she headed for the door.

Outside, Nina breathed a sigh of relief. She didn't want to be near those girls for another second! She was heading for the cafeteria when her friends rushed up to her.

"Hi, guys!" she started. "How'd you know where I—"

Mollie had a smug expression on her face. Opening the Spy Society compact, she swiped the powder like a wheel. Suddenly Nina was listening to the conversation she'd just had in the bathroom!

"Way to go, super sleuth," Tatum congratulated. "I think you just figured out how that trench coat works!"

"Holy moly," Nina replied, taking it all in. "This is serious spy gear!"

"It certainly is," Tatum agreed. "And we're getting seriously good at using it!"

The girls huddled together. "Just wait until I show you what this does," Mollie told Nina, holding up the lip-gloss camera. "We caught Mabel in the act with it!"

"In the act of what?" Nina asked.

Brrriiiinnngggg! The ten-minute bell echoed loudly in the hall. "Already?" Mollie said, frowning.

"I haven't even eaten!" Nina moaned.

"I'll have to tell you the rest later, but one thing is for sure," Mollie said. "There's a lot more intrigue at Lincoln Middle School than we thought!"

Chapter 7

"HURRY!" CAMILLE whispered, her eyes alight with excitement. "I need to get you in here before Mr. York finds out I'm not too sick to be at rehearsal!" She gazed at the clock at the end of the hall through her oversized sunglasses. "I can barely see through these things!" She giggled, then changed character completely. "The hour for covert operation number seven has come. The coast is clear. Agent M, report for adventure."

Mollie rolled her eyes, but couldn't stifle a grin. Having Camille around made everything more exciting!

"Do you have the necessary equipment?" Camille asked.

Mollie held up the MP3 player. "Check," she replied.

"Excellent. Please get into position."

Mollie took a deep breath. "Here it goes," she murmured. She stepped into her locker, wiggled herself in among the hooks and books, and turned to face front.

"Wow, you fit amazingly well in there," Camille said, breaking character and smiling admiringly.

"It's not as comfy as it looks!" Mollie said, wincing. She put one of the earbuds in her ear, making sure it wasn't tangled up on any locker stuff. "But I'm as ready as I'll ever be. You'd better close the door before I change my mind . . . or someone sees us!"

Camille nodded, back in spy mode. "Right. Okay, Agent M. Good mission, and good luck! I'll be keeping watch from my secret post and will spring you from this metal box as soon as our mission is complete." Camille closed the door, and the locker was instantly dark. The only light Mollie could see came through the narrow vents just above eye level. She listened to Camille's receding footsteps, then . . . nothing.

Mollie tried to stay still in the cramped space. Her

arm fell asleep in no time—it felt like tiny needles were pricking it. She adjusted her position as quietly as she could.

Why did I think this was a good idea? she wondered. Her hip was starting to ache. *Oh wait, I didn't,* she remembered. *Camille did!* And for good reason. Travis Brandt—the guy they saw arguing with Mabel—and his buddy Frank Gorge always came by their lockers after football practice, and their lockers were across the hall from Mollie's. Plus the school was practically deserted by four thirty. That meant it would be extra-easy to overhear a conversation . . . especially with the right gear.

Mollie adjusted the earbud and made sure the MP3 player was ready. But before she even pressed the button, she heard something. Footsteps, coming closer. And something jangling.

Ignoring her aching limbs, Mollie held perfectly still. Then she recognized the sound. It was Mr. Howard, the janitor, coming down the hall.

She adjusted her leg, barely tapping the door. A crack

of light grew wider at the bottom of the locker. Camille hadn't latched the door! The jangling noise came closer. And closer. Mollie shut her eyes. Suddenly the jangling stopped. It was right outside her locker!

"Kids need to be more careful," Mr. Howard muttered, jiggling the door handle.

Oh no! Mollie opened her eyes and held her breath. A bright light flashed across her face. The door was open!

Mollie caught a glimpse of Mr. Howard's arm, and the dust mop handle. She waited breathlessly for him to see her, to yank her out of there and . . .

Slam! The door closed and the jangling keys began to move away.

Mollie's heart thudded in her chest. She gasped for air, feeling claustrophobic. That was too close. *Let me out of here!* she shouted in her head.

"There's no way out," someone replied. "It's totally locked down."

What? Mollie shook her head, confused. She didn't usually talk back to herself. Wait, hold on. That wasn't her voice! It was a boy's. . . .

It was Frank Gorge's.

Mollie took a deep breath and reminded herself that she'd been waiting to hear this voice all along. That was why she was in here! Now that the halls were empty, she didn't really need the MP3 to hear. What she needed was something to record with! She wished she were wearing Nina's trench coat so she could record with it. That would give them actual evidence. Duh! Why hadn't they thought of that? They were pretty green at the spy stuff, no matter how good Camille was at pretending to be a pro.

Suddenly she remembered that her cell phone could record. It wasn't spy gear, but in the quiet hallway it would probably be enough. She reached for it, banging her funny bone as she pressed "record."

"Ouch!" she said before she could stop herself.

"Dude, I didn't even touch you," Travis said.

"What?" Frank grumbled.

Mollie tensed and tried to stay very still. The moment passed, and the boys returned to the conversation they'd been having before Mollie's yelp.

"Dude, you're starting to lose it," Frank said. "Don't worry. We're taking care of everything. Right?"

"That's right. I got it all set up," Travis agreed. "Saturday night is the night. Mabel is on board after some, um, negotiating." Even stuck inside her locker, Mollie could hear the smirk in Travis's voice. It made the hair on the back of her neck stand up.

"We'll be sitting pretty before we know it," Travis said.

Two locker doors banged closed, and the guys headed out. When all was quiet again, she hit "stop" on her phone. A moment later she heard light footsteps, and Camille opened the door.

Mollie squinted in the bright light. "Am I glad to see you," she said, stepping out into a massive a stretch. She rubbed her aching elbow.

"Did you get anything?" Camille asked, her eyes wide.

Mollie blew an auburn corkscrew out of her eyes. "I think so. But it's hard to say," she admitted. "As far as I can tell, seventh-grade boys speak in code!"

Chapter 8

TATUM SAT with Nina and Camille in first period math, tapping the "broken" pen—that came with the notebook—on her desk. The girls had a Spy Society meeting scheduled for after school. But at the moment, that seemed like a million years away.

In front of the class, Mr. Rasheed was rambling on about rounding decimals. Rounding decimals wasn't tricky for Tatum, so she wasn't really paying attention. Her mind was going in ten different directions at once . . . all having to do with the weird stuff that was happening at school.

More than anything, Tatum wanted to put all the

evidence the Spy Society had gathered together to see if it made any sense. It felt like their clues were tiny puzzle pieces strewn across a giant table . . . and it wasn't clear if they'd even come from the same box.

With a sigh, Tatum gave the spy pen a final tap and switched to a real pen. She was jotting down what Mr. Rasheed had written on the board when the ancient school intercom crackled to life.

"Good morning, students, this is your principal, Ms. Stern," the voice said. "I trust you slept well last night and ate a good breakfast in preparation for your school day. As you know, it is testing time. We are approaching the end of the marking period, which means enough sleep and good nutrition are especially important.

"I am certain," the principal went on, "that I don't need to remind any of you that a three-point-three grade point average is required for all students to continue with their extracurricular activities."

Tatum exchanged a look with Nina. She wasn't sure which was harder to listen to, the crackling intercom or the principal's lecture. They'd all heard it a dozen times!

Nina was shrugging in response when Ms. Stern paused and the quiet crackling of the intercom lingered in the silent classroom. After a loud exhalation, Ms. Stern cleared her throat.

"While the student body has been doing quite well overall, I have noticed *remarkable* improvements in the grades of some students here at Lincoln."

Camille raised an eyebrow in Nina's direction.

"If those grades have been studied for and achieved honestly, they are commendable. If, however, I find a student has not *earned* his or her *own* grade, the infraction will be handled quite seriously."

Tatum heard the suspicion in the principal's voice loud and clear. Judging by the looks on her friends' faces, they did, too. Ms. Stern thought people were cheating! The Spy Society knew it!

"Thank you, students and teachers," the principal said. "You may now get back to the hard work of learning."

The intercom clicked off, and everyone started talking at once. Tatum felt a little jolt of excitement—

that announcement was definitely a sign that they were onto something! While Mr. Rasheed tried to get his class to refocus on his lesson, Tatum pulled out her spy notebook and wrote a list using the special pen. When it was finished she discreetly passed it to Camille, who slipped on the sunglasses to read.

Clues:
- Mabel cheated on a math test
- Nerd Herders suddenly invited to Bubble Gum parties
- Travis overheard intimidating Mabel

Questions:
- Who is Mabel cheating for?
- Who else is involved?
- Why are the Nerd Herders getting party invites?

Suspicious Persons:
- Travis Brandt! He needs the grades to stay in sports.
- Other Sports Pack members?
- The Bubble Gums?

Tatum watched Camille read the notes, waiting for a reaction. Camille's eyes were huge when she removed the sunglasses to pass them—and the notebook—to Nina. Nina had just slipped on the magic shades when their teacher, Mr. Rasheed, suddenly appeared beside Nina's desk. In a flash he had confiscated both items.

"Passing notes, ladies?" he asked. "Did you not hear what Ms. Stern just said?" He shook his head, clearly disappointed. "I don't expect this kind of behavior from you, Ms. Crandall."

Tatum was feeling like an idiot when Camille spoke up. "Oh no, Mr. Rasheed. We weren't passing notes. Nina just needed some paper, so I gave her some."

Looking skeptical, Mr. Rasheed scowled before opening the notebook and thumbing through the pages. Tatum's heart pounded, even though she knew the notebook appeared to be blank. What if the writing suddenly became visible?

Mr. Rasheed cleared his throat and snapped the notebook shut, setting it on Nina's desk. "My apologies," he said simply. "I appear to have been mistaken."

Chapter 9

"ALL RIGHT," Camille said, turning on her heel. She was pacing the room in front of her friends, who sat on her bed. Spy Society meeting time had arrived at last. "What do we have so far?" she asked, tightening the sash on her mother's trench coat. "Agent T, as operation leader, you should report first."

Tatum looked a little surprised at being named operation leader, but regained her composure, smoothing a dark curl at her temple. "Most of you read through my notes from this morning's math class," she began.

"And she doesn't mean math notes!" Nina said with a laugh, adjusting the fedora she'd borrowed from her dad.

"I haven't," Mollie said, looking slightly put out.

Tatum pulled out the notebook while Camille handed over the glasses.

"We almost got totally busted by Mr. Rasheed," Nina explained.

"Thank goodness for invisible ink," Tatum laughed. She opened the book and handed it to Mollie.

Mollie scanned through the notes. "Do we have anything new to add?"

"Well, this could be nothing," Tatum offered. "But when Coach Howl warned everyone about keeping their grades up at volleyball practice yesterday, every Sports Packer there pretty much laughed it off."

"Do you think Coach Howl is in on the cheating?" Camille asked breathlessly, her mouth open in an O.

Tatum patted Camille's arm soothingly and shook her head. "No, I don't think so. But the laughing answers one of our questions—it looks like the whole Sports Pack, and not just Travis, is in on the cheating. And we know where the answers are coming from. We have pictures. Agent M?"

Clearing her throat, Mollie turned her laptop to face her friends. The picture of Mabel's extra test was on the screen.

"Mabel is either copying tests or taking them for other students. Look," she pointed out. "This paper even has a name on it."

The girls all squinted at the screen. Mabel's hand was covering most of it, but the name ended in a *t*.

"Travis Brandt?" Mollie suggested, raising her eyebrows. "And listen to this." She pressed "play" on her phone. Frank's and Travis's voices, a little muffled, filled the room.

"Saturday night is the night. Mabel is on board after some, um, negotiating."

"Saturday night," Tatum repeated. "On Saturday night something will be going on with Travis, Frank, and Mabel . . . maybe at Kayla's big party?"

"It has to be," Mollie agreed.

"Wait, where were you when you recorded this?" Nina interrupted. "It's like you're right next to them."

Mollie rolled her eyes. "In my locker!" she admitted.

Tatum gave Mollie a pat on the back. "Good one."

"My idea." Camille beamed. "I knew that Frank and Travis would come by like they always do. But we needed the compact-sized Agent M to pull it off." She tightened her belt again. "Anything else, agents?"

Nina leaned in to reread the notes over Mollie's shoulder. "I think we can cross the Bubble Gums off the list of suspects," she said. "The whole thing with the party invites is weird, but when I heard Kayla and Hilary in the bathroom they didn't sound worried about grades. I think they just want to show off for everyone."

"But the Bubble Gums don't usually care what the Herd thinks. Why are they including them now? And Mabel certainly didn't look happy to be invited." Suddenly Tatum's expression changed. "Maybe . . ."

"Maybe what?" Camille urged.

"Maybe somebody wants the Herd there for other reasons," Tatum said. "Maybe the Bubble Gums invited them because the Sports Pack asked them to."

"Right! Maybe they want to get Mabel and her friends away from school so they can put the pressure on! Or maybe they'll even be getting test answers!" Camille gasped.

Nina shivered in her trench. "Something's going down at that party, that's for sure! It looks like the jocks are bullying the smart kids into cheating so they can get good grades. . . ."

"Right. But how are we going to prove it?" Tatum asked.

"We have to get into Kayla's party," Camille decided.

"We have to record the Sports Packers harassing the Nerd Herders, or get pictures of the Herders handing off answers. But we can't be obvious. Agents N and M should go, I think. M is intimately familiar with the compact. And N's fashion sense will ensure you both look better than anyone on the guest list." Camille nodded decisively.

Nina dusted off her hands, patted Mollie on the back, and stood up, ready for action. "Kayla's birthday party, here we come!" she announced.

Chapter 10

"I CAN'T believe we're doing this," Mollie said nervously, as she followed Nina up the sloping drive to Kayla's large colonial-style house.

"I know. Even the house looks intimidating," Nina agreed. Towering over them, the two-story brick house was lit up like Las Vegas. Music blared and Nina could see groups of twos and threes heading toward the front door. Nina stole a look at her friend, grabbed her arm, and pulled her into the bushes.

"Hey!" Mollie protested.

"Resistance is futile," Nina said, quickly assessing her spy partner's outfit in the light cast by the house—a few touch-ups from her, and Mollie would be practically invisible. "We need to make some adjustments." She tugged at Mollie's collar and shoved a hat over her red curls. Dabbing gloss (the real kind) onto her lips, she pretended not to notice her friend's grimace.

"Do you have to do this?" Mollie asked. "Can't I catch the jocks in the act without getting all . . . dolled up?"

Nina briskly swiped mascara across Mollie's lashes and nodded emphatically. "Part of being invisible is looking like them. They'll eat you alive if you look too young."

Mollie sighed and wiped the gloss off her lips with the back of her hand. "They're not monsters; they're just . . . seventh graders."

"Right, and we're sixth graders. And it's our job to fit in at their party, or we'll never get the info we need," Nina explained.

Mollie's green eyes flickered with doubt. She spent enough time with older kids to know that she definitely did *not* fit in. "Easy for you—you're taller than most of them."

Nina grinned. "True. But if you keep your curls under that hat, your micro size will make it easier for *you* to blend. That's why you are going to be the primary mobile investigator. And why you need this . . ."

Nina unbuttoned her trench coat and held it open for Mollie to slip into.

"What? You're kidding, right? That coat is way too long for me. I'll look like I'm in kindergarten!"

Nina ignored her and put the coat on Mollie.

"This is ridiculous," Mollie protested, looking down at the way-too-long trench.

"Hold on a sec." Nina rolled up the sleeves and cinched the belt, making the coat a little shorter. But it was still almost down to Mollie's ankles. "It's fine," Nina insisted. "Rather stylish, in fact."

"My turn," Mollie said, handing the compact to Nina. "So you can hear me," she explained. "When I cry for help."

"You're going to be totally fine," Nina said encouragingly. "That coat is amazing, and so are you. You just need one final item. . . ." She reached into the

Spy Society bag, pulled out Camille's sunglasses, and slipped them onto Mollie's nose. Then, without giving Mollie another minute to protest, she grabbed her arm and dragged her back onto the walk. "Ready?" Nina asked.

"Ready," Mollie agreed, stumbling a little. "As I'll ever be," Nina heard her add under her breath.

Picking up the pace, Nina steered Mollie into a pack of girls. Two minutes later they were sliding into the party unnoticed. "We have to make sure we see Kayla and Hilary before they see us so we don't get caught," Nina advised.

Mollie nodded, gazing around. "Right, except it's a little hard to see anything with these things on."

"Don't worry, you'll get used to it." Nina gripped Mollie's arm tighter. "Now you just have to locate a Pack member or a Nerd Herder and stick to them like glue. Hey! Is that Travis?" she whispered excitedly.

"Where?" Mollie asked.

"There!" Nina leaned forward to get a better view. "I think it's him." She gave Mollie a little shove, and she lurched forward, knocking into someone's nachos.

"Hey, get your own!" the girl protested, steadying her plate.

Nina watched as Mollie mumbled something and walked away with her hands out in front of her like a blind person. Then some guys she barely recognized blocked her view. The place was packed!

Stepping into a corner, Nina pulled out the compact and prepared to receive transmissions from Mollie's trench coat. She held it securely in her hand while she wandered around, trying to act nonchalant. There were several grown-ups in the kitchen, filling platters with chicken. The living room was decorated with so many black and white streamers, you could barely see the ceiling, and giant cupcake towers were piled on every table.

Nina paused to watch the DJ Kayla had hired. She had to admit, he looked like he knew what he was doing. The music was thumping and the dance floor was crammed full of kids. Nina was tapping along to the beat when she got caught in a tangle of girls rushing the dance floor.

Oh no! she thought. Everyone around her was moving to the music. *I look like a total weirdo when I dance!* She stood perfectly still, wondering what to do and feeling like a complete idiot.

"Are you going to dance, or what?" a boy next to her shouted over the music. He was flailing his arms and stepping from one foot to the other with incredible speed. Then, all of a sudden he hip checked her, hard.

Luckily Nina caught herself before she did a public lip skid. But the Spy Society compact flew out of her hand. All Nina could do was watch helplessly as it skittered across the crowded floor.

Chapter 11

MOLLIE GRABBED the handrail and started up the stairs. "Heading to the second floor," she said into the trench collar. "No sign of Travis yet."

She hoped she would have more luck locating suspects away from the chaos. Maybe Travis and his pals wanted a quieter, private place to put pressure on the Herd. Clutching the banister, she let the smooth wood under her palm guide her. Behind the dark glasses she was practically blind. *I don't know how Camille can walk around in these,* she thought, squinting to make out faces.

Mollie reached the top and turned down the hall.

Seventh graders were hanging out all over the house. There seemed to be a crowd in every room. She could feel the music thumping through the floor. Moving slowly so she wouldn't crash into anyone, she stepped into a game room where a handful of kids were playing air hockey and foosball.

She strained her eyes in search of Sports Packers. Aside from Nina's possible Travis sighting, she hadn't seen any yet, which was weird. It definitely had sounded like they were coming.

"Score!" someone at the foosball table shouted.

"You shot it into my goal, dork brain." His competitor laughed.

Nope, Mollie thought. *Definitely not Sports Packers.* "No sportos up here," Mollie reported. "No brains up here, either," she noted, feeling foolish.

Mollie had to maneuver through a cluster of boys in the hall to get to the next room—a bedroom. She stepped inside, relieved to be in a quieter space.

"No one in the master bedroom," she reported. It was so nice to be alone Mollie was tempted to sit for a second, but she had work to do. She was on her way out when a group of Sports Packers came through the door, laughing hysterically. Finally!

Thinking fast, Mollie stepped into the closet and pulled the door almost closed behind her.

Plunged into darkness, she was feeling a little panicky when she realized that she could actually see just fine. "What the heck?" she mumbled to the shelves of sweaters and shoes. Then it dawned on her . . . the sunglasses she was wearing doubled as night vision glasses!

Duh! she thought, reaching up to feel for the dial. She'd completely forgotten about the dial! She turned it, and everything went black.

"I'm such a dork," she quietly confessed into her collar. She turned the dial back so she could see again and peeked through the crack at the pack of girls in the bedroom. She recognized several volleyball players from Nina and Tatum's team. Their laughter had died off and they were whispering to one another earnestly.

"We need to get to Val's," one of them said.

Val's? Mollie thought. Why would they want to go out for mediocre pizza when there was a ton of food right downstairs?

"I don't want the Pack to start without us," someone added.

Another girl Mollie didn't recognize nodded. "I know, but I had to see what Kayla's been bragging about."

"Me, too, but it's getting late. I don't want to make Travis mad—the Pack has to stick together on this. Plus we don't want to miss the brain spilling."

Mollie felt a tingle snake up her spine. *Brain spilling??* That didn't sound good!

"No, we don't!" the first girl agreed. "In fact, I'd say we want to be there for as much brain spilling as possible!"

"Right. Let's go!"

The Pack rushed the door. One of the girls stumbled on the rug, catching herself on the closet door. Mollie jumped back as the closet slammed shut.

Thank goodness she didn't knock it open instead! Mollie thought while she waited for them to leave. "I'm coming down," she whispered to Nina. "We've got to follow the Sports Packers!"

She adjusted the dial on her glasses so she'd be able to see in the light and then reached for the door handle. Only the handle didn't turn—it was locked!

Chapter 12

"OUCH!" NINA squealed and hopped up and down on her uninjured foot. The other one throbbed. Apparently she was not the only one at Kayla's party who lacked grace and coordination. The dance floor was a total hazard! But there was no getting off of it until she recovered the Spy Society compact.

Nina searched the floor and tried not to panic. The gear had to be here.

There! Nina spotted the round case surrounded by a circle of bopping girls. She lunged toward it, reached out her arm, and—

Dang. Somebody in supercute sparkly ballet flats

kicked the compact. It skittered farther across the floor.

"'Scuse me. Pardon me." Nina squeezed through the throng. She hoped that when she finally got her hands on the compact it would still be functional. There was no telling how many times it had been kicked, or worse!

"Gotcha!" Nina dove between a pair of high-tops and some seriously buckled boots and felt her fingers graze the case. Half a second later it slipped farther away. Frantic, Nina did a crazy crawl past a kid doing the chicken and two girls bumping hips. She reached . . .

Phew! Her hand closed firmly around the compact. Nina stood up with as much dignity as she could, tossing her hair over a shoulder. She slid the device into her pocket. *Please work. Please work. Please work,* she thought as she moved off the dance floor.

Safe in a quietish corner, Nina took the compact out and opened it up. The mirror wasn't broken. That was good. No seven years' bad luck or whatever. But why couldn't she hear anything? She ran her finger around the part where powder was usually packed, trying to tune Mollie in. It was hard to hear over the party noise, but there was a soft crackling and then . . .

"What the . . . ?! Whoa!" Not only was the mirror intact; it was more than a mirror. Way more! The circle flickered, and suddenly Nina was looking at several Sports Pack girls huddled together. Only where was Mollie?

Nina spun the wheel again and the picture disappeared. There was a soft crackling. She found the volume and turned it to max, holding it up to her ear.

". . . apped in the closet!"

What?

"Upstairs in the master bedroom. Can you hear me? I need help! I can't get out!" It was Mollie's voice, all right. And she was freaking out!

"I'm on my way," Nina said, even though Mollie couldn't hear her. She shimmied across the dance floor without injury and raced for the stairs. *Upstairs bedroom*, she repeated to herself, opening door after door and peeking in.

Office.

Game room.

Bathroom.

"Sorry!" Nina called to the surprised occupant behind door number three. So much for being discreet.

The fourth door had to lead to the room she was looking for. Inside, it looked like the room she had seen on the compact screen, only without the Sports Pack in it. "Mollie?" Nina whispered.

"In here!" Mollie rattled the closet doorknob.

Nina yanked open the closet door, and a very rosy Mollie, still wrapped in the too-big trench and wearing the glasses, stumbled out.

"Oh my gosh. That's the second time this week I've been locked in a tiny space," Mollie panted, fanning her face. "I think I'm developing claustrophobia!"

Nina was thrilled to see Mollie, but her eyes were drawn to something else. Kayla's mom had great taste . . . the closet was filled with amazing designer dresses!

"Would you *look* at this?" Nina pulled down a dress and held it up to her shoulders. "These are amazing! Do you think this would fit me?"

"Forget the clothes," Mollie snapped. "Try this on for

size: As far as I can tell, there is not a single member of the Nerd Herd here."

Nina reluctantly hung the dress back up. There was urgency in Mollie's voice, and they *were* on a mission.

"There were a few Sports Pack girls here before I got stuck in the closet."

"I saw," Nina said. She opened the compact and played back the video.

"Whoa! I didn't know they could do that!" Mollie touched the glasses. Then she shook her head. "We gotta get to Val's."

Now Nina was confused. "But there's pizza and stuff downstairs," she said.

"Didn't you hear? They aren't after pizza. They were talking about 'spilling brains.'"

"Holy moly!" Nina gasped, putting it all together. "That's why none of the Herd is here. The Pack must have them cornered at Val's!"

Nina and Mollie raced into the hall and pounded down the stairs. They were almost at the bottom when Nina stopped short and Mollie squashed her nose into her friend's back. "Whmph."

Kayla and Hilary were standing between them and the way out, right next to an elaborate punch bowl. Their glossy lips were twisted into angry pouts, and they were chewing their gum furiously.

"Oooh, they look mad," Mollie whispered.

With their backs to the table, Mollie and Nina tried to slide past the exit. On the way they strained to catch what the Bubble Gums were saying.

"I can't believe those geeks didn't even show!" Kayla whined.

"And the Sports Pack! I mean, we went through all this trouble to throw the party of the year, and for them to not even come? It's insulting!" Hilary complained, planting her hands on her hips.

Still moving backward, Nina tried to squeeze between the drink table and the wall so she could make her escape. She was skinny enough to do it, but halfway through she stumbled and knocked the table. A wave of sticky red liquid sloshed out of the bowl and all over Hilary's and Kayla's beautiful black-and-white outfits.

"Ewww!" Kayla squealed.

Everyone turned to look . . . at Nina and Mollie, sixth-grade interlopers!

"Let's go." Mollie pushed past Nina, grabbing her hand and yanking her along. Nina did not need to be told twice. The sooner they got out of the sticky situation, the better.

Ignoring the angry stares of a million popular seventh graders, Mollie and Nina flew through the door and down the sidewalk.

Even with her short legs, Mollie was making good time.

"How can you move so fast in the dark?" Nina gasped. She was groping her way along, hoping not to fall flat on her face yet again.

Mollie slowed. She grinned at Nina and tapped her glasses. "Night vision." She beamed. "Now come on. We've got to get to Val's!"

Chapter 13

TATUM STARED at her phone wishing she could *make* it ring. She and Camille were sitting in Camille's room waiting to hear from Nina and Mollie.

"I knew we should have kept the compact!" Tatum complained. Beside her, Camille bounced. She was full of nervous energy.

Tatum could have done some bouncing herself. She reread the last text she'd sent: *R U in?* "Why aren't they texting us back? I wish they would just call!" she moaned.

And just like that the phone rang. Tatum pushed the speakerphone button before the ringtone could play through. "Hello?"

The girls heard panting on the line. "Hey," Mollie gasped. "Nobody . . . at the . . . party."

"Nobody?" Tatum was having trouble picturing that.

"No nerds, no sportos," Mollie replied. "Just Bubble Gums. Gotta . . . get to . . . Val's," she went on between breaths. "Could be . . . trouble."

The phone beeped and a *Call Failed* message flashed on the screen. "Dang it!" Tatum shoved the phone in her pocket. Camille was headed out the door. "Wait up!" she called after her. But Camille was already playing a new role—action hero—and leaping down the steps.

Tatum caught up to Camille in the garage, straddling her bike. "That's for you," Camille said. She pointed at a teeny pink bike with handlebar tassels—her little sister Lola's bike—before rolling out of the driveway.

At least it doesn't have training wheels, Tatum thought, looking at the candy-colored bike. But it *was* about three sizes too small. Tatum climbed on and pedaled after Camille with her knees making circles near her ears. *I must look like a clown*, she thought. But this was no time for pride. Camille was already disappearing in the distance.

Awkwardly making her way toward Val's, Tatum wished she'd gotten more info from Mollie. She understood that the Nerd Herd and Sports Pack kids had not shown up at the party. What she didn't understand was why they were all at Val's . . . unless Travis and his friends were trying to lure the brainiacs away so they could push them around with fewer witnesses.

The thought made Tatum's blood run cold. She and her friends could be headed into a serious situation. But it could be their best chance to catch the jocks red-handed. Picturing meek Mabel and her spindly pals facing off against the biggest, strongest seventh graders in the school made Tatum's stomach flip-flop. She pedaled faster.

Two turns later, Tatum saw the Val's sign lighting up the dark sky. Camille's bike was on its side near the double doors, tires still spinning. "Hang on, Camille," Tatum called. She dumped the bike and sprinted into the restaurant foyer.

Camille was standing with the newspaper and bubble-gum machines, waiting. *Phew!* She had the MP3 player out and was holding it to the solid door leading into Val's. She held one of the earbuds out to Tatum. "Listen," she hissed.

Tatum put in the bud. A voice came through loud and clear. . . .

". . . split into pieces," Tatum heard. Her eyes grew wider. It was Travis's voice!

"Teeny, tiny pieces," said another voice.

Frank!

"No. Stop. Hold on." It was a girl's voice this time. It had to be Mabel. And she was pleading with them!

"Forget evidence," Tatum said, ripping out the earphone. "We have to help!"

She and Camille pushed the doors open and burst into the dark pizza parlor like Charlie's Angels, ready to take on Mabel's attackers!

Only what they saw was not exactly a torture scene.

"Oh my gosh." Camille put her hand to her mouth, speechless.

Tatum looked around at the tables of Nerd Herders and Sports Packers. They were leaning over open books.

They were surrounded by calculators and scratch paper. This was not a rumble. It was a cram session. Yes, the Nerd Herd was helping the Sports Pack with their grades, but not by cheating. They were helping them STUDY!

Tatum's face felt hot. Before she could get too embarrassed, Nina and Mollie stumbled in, puffing like steam trains.

"Mabel, are you okay?" Nina cried.

As all eyes in the restaurant turned to focus on the four flustered girls by the entrance, Mabel shrugged. "Sure," she said. "Bisecting triangles is easy."

Chapter 14

MOLLIE GOT out of bed on Monday wondering if she had slept at all. After the discovery at Val's and the sleepover at Camille's, she was exhausted! But she also felt better than she had since the day they'd found the Spy Society bag. Victorious—the way you feel when you slide the last piece of a 1,000-piece puzzle into place and give it a tap.

As she got ready for school, she wondered if this was how real spies felt. Surely, in the spy world, losing a little sleep was no big deal. Especially when you were about to break a case wide open.

The night they'd cracked it all open had been

completely crazy. They'd raced in looking for one thing and found something totally different. A quick conversation with Mabel had cleared it up. As it turned out, there were more pieces to the cheater puzzle than they'd originally thought—and the Spy Society had been trying to put a few pieces where they didn't belong.

Now the four sleuths had to tell Principal Stern exactly what they'd found out. That made Mollie more nervous than hiding in a locker or sneaking into a seventh-grade party . . . way more!

Mollie's stomach fluttered as she got off the bus at school. She wished for the thirty-seventh time this year that one of her friends shared her bus route. She scanned the quad for her fellow spies, but nobody was milling on the yard.

In fact, nobody was milling anywhere. The air was electric and teachers were directing everyone into the gym for an emergency assembly. Something was up.

Inside the gym, the bleachers were filled with buzzing students. Mollie spotted Tatum and the others about five rows up and began to make her way through the crowd. She wasn't quite there when the bell rang, and Principal Stern spoke into the mic set up in front.

"Take your seats," the principal ordered.

Mollie almost sat down right where she was. Ms. Stern sounded even more like her name than usual.

"Lincoln students, I am very disappointed," the principal said. She was scowling so hard it looked like her eyebrows were shaking hands. "Last week I began to suspect something strange was going on at our school. I didn't want to believe it, but the evidence was striking. Over the weekend I dug a little deeper."

"She wasn't the only one," Mollie whispered, reaching her friends. She slipped into the spot Nina had saved for her.

"What I discovered made me more than suspicious," Ms. Stern said. "Sharp spikes in grades are one thing, but when students get identical marks, it is clear that there is something dishonest going on." She was staring down the entire gymnasium!

Mollie sat on her hands and bit her lip while Ms. Stern lectured them about integrity. And honesty. And fairness. Farther down the row, Tatum was writing in the spy notebook. She finished writing and passed the book and sunglasses to Camille. Mollie saw Camille gulp before she passed the spy stuff to Nina. Finally it was Mollie's turn.

We should say something NOW, it read.

"Is there anyone here who has something to say?" the principal barked, making Mollie start. Was she reading over her shoulder?

Mollie glanced at Mabel, who looked like she might faint. She located Travis and Frank in the crowd—they were both looking sheepish and studying something on the floor. The Bubble Gums, on the other hand, were chatting, texting, and ignoring the whole scene.

Mollie's blood boiled. Before she could get nervous, she stood up. "We have something to say," she blurted. She turned to her friends, who looked completely shocked. But a moment later they were standing by her side.

Moving toward the podium, the Spy Society was locked in step.

Facing the entire student body made Mollie's head spin.

"We have something to say," she repeated into the microphone.

Principal Stern looked confused. "None of you girls are under suspicion," she said.

"We know—we're not the cheaters," Mollie agreed. "But we have information that will clear all of this up." Mollie's gaze found Mabel when she said the last part. She wanted her to know she had her back.

Mollie took a deep breath. "Yes, there is a cheating ring at Lincoln. Or at least there was." Her voice quavered. "The Sports Pack was getting answers from the Nerd Herd so they could make good grades and keep playing. But before you blame the Nerd Herd or even the Sports Pack for what's been going on, you should take a closer look."

While the audience murmured in surprise, Mollie passed the mic to Tatum. "If you check the books, you might find that the Bubble Gum crowd has also gotten surprisingly smarter . . . and—"

"Wait!" Camille stepped toward Tatum and the mic. "May I?"

"Of course." Tatum handed Camille the mic with a little bow. Camille took it and turned toward the audience.

"It was a dark and stormy night when Hilary Black first cornered Mabel Brodie and invited her to a pool party," she said dramatically. "Mabel was thrilled, at first. . . ." Camille paced and eyed the bleacher crowd like a detective.

"She thought she was making new friends. Until she found her backpack missing. The Bubble Gums stole her homework, copied it, and then threatened to tell the principal that *she* was the cheater." Camille let her mouth hang open, in horror.

"They blackmailed Mabel, and then they did the same to the other nerds, too. They told Mabel and her friends they'd turn *them* in for cheating if anyone breathed a word. And they demanded more answers just to keep quiet!" Acting too horrified to continue, Camille handed the microphone to Nina.

After a quick toss of her hair, Nina continued. "So we know Mabel and her friends were tricked. But that doesn't explain how the Sports Pack was getting the answers, does it?" Nina asked. "It also doesn't explain how the Bubble Gums' party budget kept growing. You see, Kayla and Hilary didn't just use the answers they stole; they actually *sold* answers to the Sports Pack. And once someone cheated, or found out about the cheating, the Bubble Gums threatened to expose them if they told. Everyone had to play by their rules!"

The students were silent. Even Principal Stern looked shocked.

"That is, until Travis Brandt came up with a new plan," Nina continued. "He asked Mabel and her friends to help him and his friends study—to get their grades up the right way. They cut the Bubble Gums out of their own game. Nothing to hide. Nothing to be caught for." Nina shrugged.

Mollie noticed that a bit of color had come back into Mabel's face as Nina spoke. For a long minute after their tall friend finished speaking, the gym was silent. Then Principal Stern took the mic.

The principal inhaled and exhaled several times before rattling off a list of names—people she needed to see in her office right away. Mollie hid a smile when Kayla's and Hilary's names topped the list.

"I knew we had a cheating problem, but this appears to be a professional operation!" Principal Stern said, shaking her head. "I am shocked. But I am also encouraged that so many of you were trying to make the right choices under difficult circumstances. And I think we, as a community, owe a big thank-you to these . . . this . . ."

Mollie grinned. "Spy Society," she said quietly.

Principal Stern blinked in surprise, as though she wasn't sure she'd heard correctly. She put her hand over the mic. "The what?" she asked.

"Spy Society," the four girls chorused.

". . . for helping us get to the bottom of things," the principal finished before dismissing the group and switching off the mic.

"Rest assured, I'll be contacting the Spy Society if the need arises in the future," Principal Stern said, looking each of them in the eye. Then, with a wink and a rare smile, she turned on her heel and disappeared out the door.

Chapter 15

TALLULAH PULLED on the leash in Camille's hand. Her tail was wagging so fast it was a blur, and she had a huge doggie smile on her face. Camille knew just how her pup felt. It was great to be in the sunshine with her friends.

Just as Nina had predicted, all four girls had landed solidly in 3.3 GPA land. They could keep their extracurriculars! To celebrate, the Spy Society decided to take the day off. Nina shed her trench. Mollie left her makeup at home. Tatum wasn't writing any secret notes, and even though she was squinting in the bright sunlight, Camille was wearing the sunglasses on the top of her head (they were just too fabulous to leave at home).

The Spy Society was off duty, and it felt pretty great. Almost as great as it felt to have exposed the cheating ring at school.

Camille felt like celebrating. Dropping Tallulah's leash, she did a cartwheel in the grass and flopped down on their favorite bench. Nina plopped beside her and Tatum, and Mollie leaned against the big elm that grew nearby.

"I wonder what Hilary's and Kayla's report cards looked like," Nina mused. "I feel a little bad for them."

"Don't!" Tatum shook her head. "They're getting just what they deserve. They'll have plenty of time to bring their grades up." She smirked.

The Bubble Gums had been suspended from school for two weeks. When they came back, they'd have mandatory study hall detention for the rest of the year. Camille shook her head. There'd be no excuse for bad grades with that kind of time commitment!

"I feel bad for Frank and Travis," Mollie admitted. While the Nerd Herd had gotten off with a warning and three days' detention, the Sports Pack had been benched for two weeks because they had, at least for a little while, used the purchased answers. .

"Two weeks isn't much," Nina said. "They'll be back in the game before you know it."

Camille watched Tatum pull the notebook and pen out of her back pocket and start to jot something down.

"Hey. This is our day off, remember?" Camille teased.

Tatum slammed the book shut. "Okay, okay. Case closed," she agreed. "Can you believe we're back in the spot where we found the bag—it seems like forever ago, but it really hasn't been that long."

The girls were silent. It really did seem like ages. So much had happened!

Tatum put the book down and picked up Tallulah's tennis ball. She threw it in the grassy meadow, and the girls all spread out for a game of monkey in the middle. A minute later they were yelling and laughing and having fun. Before they knew it, the sun was getting rosy on the horizon and it was time to head home.

They were partway down the trail
remembered the notebook. "I

said, slapping her forehead.

"I'll get it," Camille offered. She jogged with Tallulah back to the bench. The book was right where Tatum had left it . . . with a leaf sticking out of the pages like a bookmark.

Slipping the sunglasses on, Camille opened to the marked page.

You've used your strength for good, and utilized crucial spy devices—knowledge, compassion, and friendship. Stick together; you'll go far.

"Oh my gosh!" she called, racing back to her friends. Her heart was pounding with excitement. "Listen!" Camille read the page aloud.

The girls were quiet as they considered the message.

Tatum took the glasses and pointed out the bold letters. "N-I-C-E W-O-R-K."

"I love it," Mollie said. "But who wrote it?"

"I wish I knew," Nina admitted. "Then I could thank her for my coat!"

The girls looked around.

Camille had that weird feeling they were being watched, like the day they'd found the bag. But this time it wasn't creepy. She spotted the same silver sports car she'd seen that day by the curb. The window was down, and behind the wheel was an elegant-looking woman wearing sunglasses identical to hers. "Look!" Camille pointed discreetly.

The girls all turned toward the street, and the mysterious woman smiled. She nodded slightly before rolling up the window and heading into traffic.

The Spy Society watched her drive away.

"Look. No license plate," Mollie pointed out.

"Another mystery." Camille sighed dramatically.

"Definitely," Tatum agreed. "But I have a feeling we're not supposed to solve this one."

"Besides, it's our day off," Nina said. Laughing, the Spy Society headed home in the fading light.

SPY *Society*

LET SLEEPING DOGS SPY

New girls,

new gadgets—

a brand-new adventure!

"How's this?" Elise Wallace asked, holding up a wicker basket with a piece of red gingham tucked inside.

"Perfect, as usual," Lily Vesper, one of her best friends, replied. The two girls were in the prop shop of the theater at their school, Proctor Middle. Another best friend, Peyton Mitchell, was with them . . . in body at least. Her head was completely buried in a script for the play she was assistant directing.

"Dorothy enters right. . . ." she mumbled, making a note in red ink.

"And goes directly to center stage!" Lily cried.

Lily was playing Dorothy in the state-of-the-art theater's inaugural production—*The Wizard of Oz*. And like the rest of the cast and crew, she was over-the-rainbow enthusiastic about it.

Just then Charlie Larsen strode through the door carrying an old-fashioned-looking suitcase under one arm and a small terrier under the other. "Special delivery," she announced, setting both down on the table.

Peyton lifted her chin toward the case. "What's this?"

Charlie shrugged. "No idea. I just found it by the main doors and figured it had to belong to the theater department."

"It's well made, that's for sure." Peyton ran her finger across the top of the case and peered at the letters stitched into the leather. "What do you suppose the *Ss* are for?"